Arizona Lucy

By
Carol Truchan-Schulte

Illustrated by Rebecca Tadema-Wielandt

Layout Designer: u-ranz

To order additional copies of this book, contact:
Xlibris Corporation
1-888-795-4274
www.Xlibris.com
Orders@Xlibris.com

Acknowledgements

Thank you

To my early readers, Sherese Grimsley and Laura Uchman.

**To James Ribbe for editing and to Janice Stickles
for all her advice and final editing.**

**To my illustrator, Rebecca Tadema-Wielandt
for helping Lucy come to life.**

**A special thanks to my family and friends
for their help and encouragement.**

**For my grandchildren: Haley, Caroline,
Emma, Ryan and Rachel.**

For my daughter Lisa, who made it all happen.

Little Lucy was no more than a tiny, gray, fuzzy ball when she was born on a warm spring day. She was the littlest kitten of all her brothers and sisters.

A girl named Lisa was learning to become an animal doctor at a hospital in Boston where Lucy was born. Lisa took special care of Lucy and decided to take her home. They became good friends. Lisa loved Lucy and Lucy loved Lisa.

As time went by, Lucy grew to be a beautiful cat, and Lisa finished school and became an animal doctor. Lucy was so happy and proud of Dr. Lisa. She danced around their little house singing, "Dr. Lisa, Dr. Lisa."

Lucy's adventures were only about to begin. Dr. Lisa had taken a job in Arizona. She told Lucy all about it. Lucy didn't really understand just how far Arizona was from Boston. She tried to be brave. "Oh, I'm not worried," said Lucy. "I've traveled in cars before."

When it came time to leave, Lucy wondered why everyone was sad. Dr. Lisa's mom, dad and brother were hugging each other and crying. Lucy wondered out loud, "What's the big deal? We're just going in the car again."

So Lucy climbed into her pet carrier and off they went. After some time, Lucy began to wonder why Dr. Lisa wasn't letting her out. Lucy noticed that Dr. Lisa was not driving because she was sitting in the seat right next to her. This car was very loud, and the drive was taking a long time, Lucy thought. "MEOW, MEOW. That always works. She'll let me out now." Lucy said.

Lucy didn't know she was on an airplane and that Dr. Lisa wasn't allowed to let her out. Dr. Lisa tried to tell Lucy not to worry because this would be a very long ride. They were flying almost all the way to the other side of the country.

   What does she mean telling me we're flying? I have no wings. I can't fly. Oh my gosh! Don't tell me, it couldn't be. Oh no! Maybe a big bird swallowed me up! No. It can't be a bird. Dr. Lisa would never let a bird swallow me. All these thoughts were running through Lucy's mind.

   "Oh MEOW MEOW," Lucy cried. "I'm so confused."

   "Don't worry, Lucy," Dr. Lisa said. "We're almost there. Soon you'll be in your new home in Arizona." Lucy thought: What is an Arizona?

As soon as they arrived, Dr. Lisa took Lucy out of her pet carrier so she could stretch and look around.

"Oh gosh! It's so hot. I can't breath. Are we in an oven?" Lucy asked as she stepped outside.

"Where are all the trees?" Lucy asked. It looks like my litter box. Could we be in a giant litter box, Lucy wondered.

It didn't take her long to realize this was no giant litter box but a beautiful new place called the desert.

13

Lucy noticed the trees didn't go away, they just looked different here. They were called cactuses and had needles instead of leaves. Lucy discovered if she got close enough to sniff them, the needles on them could stick into a cat's nose.

Once Dr. Lisa and Lucy settled into their new home, Lucy couldn't wait to start exploring all the rooms. She wondered if there were any mice or spiders to play with.

When Dr. Lisa was introducing herself to Sheri, her neighbor next door, Lucy got to meet the big white cat that lived there. Her name was Pearl. Pearl did not want to go outdoors. She did not want to get dirty. Sheri was always brushing Pearl and Pearl was always looking in the mirror.

"Oh well," Lucy said, "I know I'll find friends outside." Once again she was surprised to feel how hot it was in Arizona. The desert sand was so hot on Lucy's paws, but that didn't stop her from going outdoors.

Lucy hadn't gone far when she came face to face with a big gray cat. "Hell-o," said Lucy.

"Hell-o yourself," answered the cat. "Who are you?"

"My name is Lucy. I'm new here. I traveled all the way across the country in a big airplane," said Lucy.

"Big deal," answered the cat. This made Lucy feel sad. Then suddenly from behind the gray cat, came another cat.

"Hi Lucy, he said. My name is Bruno. Don't pay any attention to Tom. He tries to act tough." Bruno told Lucy he would take her around and teach her all about the desert. So off they went side by side.

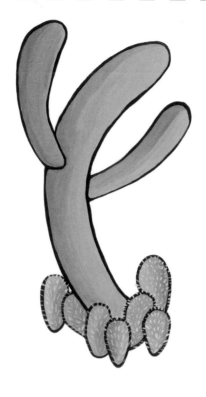

Bruno told her all about the desert plants. He told Lucy it takes about 100 years to grow an arm on a cactus plant. That's funny, Lucy thought. In Boston we call them branches on a tree.

Bruno also showed her something called a Dust Devil. Lucy was amazed. It looked like a tiny tornado. Bruno explained, "It's really little swirls of wind that go around and around sweeping the sand up like dust."

Lucy and Bruno were walking along when suddenly Lucy stopped. She yelled, "Look Bruno. It's a baby lobster. In Boston they live in the ocean. What could it be doing in the sand?"

"No, no, Lucy," said Bruno. "That's a scorpion."
Well, it is a lot smaller Lucy thought, and the color is different. Bruno went on to tell Lucy not to play with it because it was poisonous. "Oh my," Lucy said. "I think lots of things may be different here in Arizona."

Bruno and Lucy kept very still and out of the scorpion's path. Soon the scorpion disappeared into the desert. They continued on their way, chasing each other and the dust devils. Lucy was happy because she knew she had found a good friend.

As the day went on, it got hotter and hotter. Lucy and Bruno stopped playing for a while and took a nap near a cactus plant.

Lucy woke up first. She was feeling rested now and was taking a little walk by herself. She noticed a spider. It looked different from her spider friends in Boston. It was much bigger and had hairy legs. I think I'll say hell-o, thought Lucy; maybe he needs a friend too.

Just as Lucy was close enough to swat her paw at the spider,

Bruno came thundering up behind her yelling, "Nooooo Lucy!" He crashed down between her and the spider, sending Lucy spinning through the sand.

Before they knew what happened, the spider bit Bruno and ran off. "Oh no," said Bruno. "Lucy, I need help. That was a TA-RAN-CHOO-LA. He put poison into me. I feel sleepy. I feel sick."

Oh my, Lucy thought, what should I do? Bruno looked like he was sleeping. Lucy tried to wake him but couldn't. "MEOW, MEOW." Lucy began to cry.

I must run home to get Dr. Lisa, thought Lucy. When she got to the house, she jumped onto Dr. Lisa's lap and kept pawing at her sleeve. "Stop Lucy," Dr. Lisa said. "I'm reading a book. I can't play now." Lucy kept fussing and pawing at Dr. Lisa. She finally gave in and followed Lucy to the door.

Dr. Lisa continued to follow Lucy out into the back yard. She couldn't understand what Lucy wanted to show her. Lucy kept running back and forth, back and forth. Suddenly Dr. Lisa understood. Bruno was lying near a cactus tree. He seemed to be sleeping.

Dr. Lisa scooped Bruno up into her arms. She put Lucy in the house and took Bruno with her in the car. Off they went to the animal hospital. Poor Lucy watched from the window, as they drove away, tears flowing from her eyes. "MEOW, MEOW, please take me too, Dr. Lisa." Lucy cried.

It was dark outside when Dr. Lisa finally came home. She looked very tired and sad. She scooped Lucy up into her arms and began petting her. Lucy purred and cried, "MEOW, MEOW. Please take me to see Bruno." Dr. Lisa didn't know how to tell Lucy that Bruno was very sick. Several hours later and after many tests, Dr. Lisa discovered that a tarantula had bitten Bruno.

Dr. Lisa worked hard to save his life. But Bruno was still weak and very sick.

Lucy kept running to the door. She hoped Dr. Lisa understood she wanted to go to see Bruno. "Ok, Lucy. Let's give it a try. Maybe if Bruno sees you he will get better sooner," Dr. Lisa said.

Lucy was sad to see her new friend lying there so sick just because he had saved her from the awful spider. Dr. Lisa let Lucy lay close to Bruno. Lucy meowed and purred over and over, but still Bruno didn't open his eyes. Lucy was so sad. She cried and cried. Dr. Lisa left Lucy with Bruno and then went home. She hoped Lucy could help him get well just by staying close to him.

When Lucy opened her eyes the next morning, the first thing she saw was Bruno. She nuzzled up to him and said, "MEOW, MEOW." He didn't answer. "MEOW, MEOW. Wake up. Bruno, it's me, Lucy," she said. Finally, Bruno's eyes began to flutter. He saw his friend Lucy sitting next to him. He was glad to see her and happy that the TA-RAN-CHOO-LA hadn't hurt her, too.

Soon Dr. Lisa was back at the hospital checking in on Bruno and Lucy. "So Lucy," she said. "Your friend Bruno looks better today."

Each day Bruno got stronger and stronger. Both Dr. Lisa and Lucy were so happy when he was able to go home. As they left the hospital, Bruno promised Lucy they would be best friends forever.

Lucy couldn't wait to go outside to play with Bruno again. She knew he had so much more to teach her about Arizona and the desert.

Yes. Lucy loved her new best friend Bruno. Because of him, she also loved her new home, Arizona.